EMPIRE
STRIKES BACK
MISSION 2

WRITTEN BY RAITH BLACK

HENDERSON
PUBLISHING LTD

TM & © 1997 Lucasfilm Ltd.
All rights reserved.
Used under authorization.

ntent on his merciless mission to find Luke Skywalker and the Rebel base, Darth Vader sent thousands of probes deep into space. Luke was out on patrol on the ice planet, Hoth, when he saw one of the probes crash to the ice. Seen through his high-powered glasses, it looked like a meteorite. Quickly, he contacted Han Solo on the comlink. "I've finished my circle – I don't pick up any life readings. There's a meteorite that hit the ground near here. I want to check it out – it won't take long."

In the distance, he watched Han riding his tauntaun back to the base. Luke's tauntaun became edgy and reared up. "What's the matter?" Luke asked. "Can you smell something?"

Suddenly, a fierce ice creature leaped up in front of him. It swiped Luke clean off his tauntaun and dragged him away.

Back at the base, Han Solo was working on the *Millennium Falcon* when C-3PO approached him. The droid was clearly worried.

"It's Master Luke. Nobody knows where he is. He hasn't returned from patrol yet."

Han went to the departure area to check. It was true – Luke had failed to return. He decided to go out and find him, but was warned against it.

"Sir, the temperature's dropping too rapidly."

"That's right – and my friend's out in it," replied Han, undeterred.

Han must open the blast doors to get outside. Which lever must he pull?

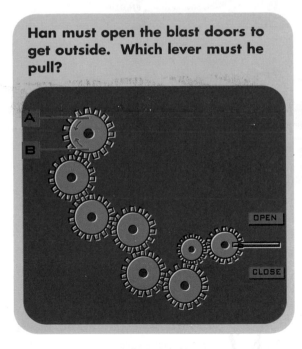

Luke woke up to find himself hanging by his feet. He looked around. He was in a cave – the ice creature's lair. On the ground nearby, he could see his lightsaber, just visible in the snow. He held out his hand and concentrated, using the Force to will the lightsaber to come to him. It shuddered and started to release.

Luke heard the ice creature shuffling towards him. He focused harder and the lightsaber flew from the snow into his waiting hand. Using the blade to free himself, he fell to the ground with a thud. When he stood up, the ice creature was upon him. He swished the lightsaber through the air and stopped the beast in its tracks. Stumbling from the cave, he could only walk a short distance before he collapsed in the snow.

The biting cold engulfed Luke. He was lying face down when a voice from nearby uttered his name. Weakly, he lifted his head and saw the image of his old friend, Obi-Wan Kenobi. "Ben?" he asked.

Obi-Wan spoke. "You will go to the Dagobah system. There you will learn from Yoda, the Jedi Master who instructed me."

The image of Obi-Wan faded. Luke called his name. "Ben? Ben?" Another figure appeared, this time riding a tauntaun. "Luke?" the rider asked. He stepped down and knelt beside him. It was Han.

Han spotted Luke on his life form scanner. He was 4 km away. If Han's tauntaun moves at 12 kph, how long will it take Han to reach Luke?

Rebel pilots swooped over the harsh landscape of Hoth, searching for Han and Luke. One of the pilots tried to contact them. "Captain Solo. Do you copy?" Han's voice crackled over the comlink. "Good morning. Nice of you guys to drop by!" The pilot hastily alerted the base. "I've found them."

Han stood up when he heard the fighter approaching. He waved at the pilot, relieved to have been found. Luke was suffering from the effects of the icy cold and needed urgent medical treatment.

As soon as they reached base, Luke was placed in a bacta tank. Medical droids administered to his body's needs.

One of the Rebel leaders reported on the situation. "We've picked something up outside the base. We intercepted this message..."

"That sounds like an Imperial code," said C-3PO.

"Chewie and I will go and check it out," volunteered Han.

Outside, Han and Chewie spotted an Imperial probe droid. Han fired at it – and the machine exploded into pieces.

"I think it self-destructed," he reported back.

"An Imperial probe droid," said Princess Leia.

"I'd lay bets that the Empire knows we're here," Han remarked, knowing it would only be a matter of time until the Empire attacked them. Leia, who had been thinking quietly to herself, made a decision.

Can you work out Leia's decision?

CODE: A = 2, B = 4, C = 6...

10/44/2/6/42/2/40/10
36/10/4/10/24
4/2/38/10

Vader was surveying the fleet from the bridge of his Destroyer when he heard his commanders discussing a signal. He strode over.

The commanders were debating about a row of circular shapes, sticking out of the ground, seen on a screen in front of them. Vader knew immediately what these shapes were. It was the moment he had been waiting for.

"That's it," he announced. "The Rebels are there. That is the system and I'm sure Skywalker is with them." He issued a command. "Set course for the Hoth system. General, prepare your men."

Looming on the horizon, the Rebel soldiers could see the threatening approach of Imperial walkers. These huge armoured machines had an awesome array of fire power, with two heavy laser cannons at the front. As they grew closer, the walkers started to blast the Rebels.

Luke led the retaliation. The Rebel forces fired their blasters, but found they were useless. "The armour's too strong for our blasters. Use your harpoons and tow cables – it might be our only chance of stopping them," he ordered.

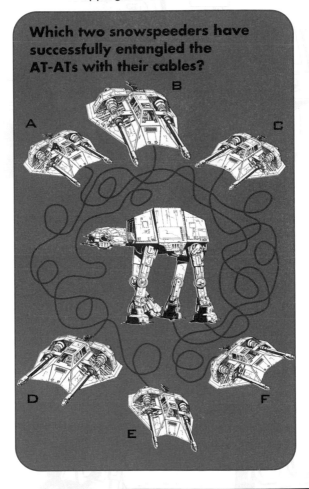

Which two snowspeeders have successfully entangled the AT-ATs with their cables?

As Luke was about to attack, his vehicle was hit
and he lost his gunner. In flew another pilot,
who fired a harpoon which attached to the legs
of the walker. Flying precariously around and
around the feet of the giant AT-AT, the pilot
entangled the towering mechanical legs. After
just a few steps, the machine began to topple
over, crashing to the ground and exploding.
Luke attacked again, but took a second hit. His
fighter crashed. He managed to escape just
before a huge robotic leg pounded his ship.
Attaching a cable to the underside of the walker,
Luke slid up to the belly. Opening a hatch, he
threw in a charge before dropping to the
ground. The interior of the Imperial walker
exploded, destroying it completely.
Inside the base, realising that the Empire was too
powerful to defeat, Leia ordered a complete
evacuation.

The commander of one of the Imperial walkers targeted the main generator of the base. Soon destroyed, he informed Vader that he could deploy the remainder of his troops.

Han grabbed Leia and dragged her away from the control room. "I'm taking you to your ship," he said.

On the way, a blast destroyed part of the base, separating Han and Leia from the ship. Han decided to escape with her on the *Millennium Falcon*. Together they ran for their lives. Behind them, Darth Vader entered the base, following his snowtroopers.

The Imperial troops arrived just as Han, Leia, Chewie and C-3PO entered the *Falcon*, but the ship failed to start. Han pounded at the controls in frustration, trying to see what was wrong. Imperial troops lined up their cannons and blasted mercilessly away at the *Falcon*. At that moment, the ominous shadow of Darth Vader appeared…but the ship spluttered into life. Still under attack, Han blasted away from the base. Vader watched angrily as the *Millennium Falcon* escaped his grasp.

L uke made his way to his X-wing which had been prepared for his evacuation. R2-D2 was in the rear. Strapping himself in, Luke set the co-ordinates. Artoo beeped at him. "There's nothing wrong, Artoo. Don't worry. We're not going to regroup with the others. We're going to the Dagobah system."

To set the co-ordinates, Luke must complete the pyramid. Each number is the sum of the two numbers below – for example,

	7 T	
3 A		4 M

The numbers also have a letter. To select the co-ordinates, match the letter to the number in the green boxes provided to spell out a word.

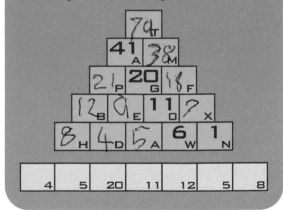

			79 T			
		41 A		38 M		
	21 P		20 G		18 F	
12 B		9 E		11 O		7 X
8 H	4 D	5 A	6 W	1 N		

4	5	20	11	12	5	8

Although the *Falcon* had escaped from Hoth, it soon came under attack. TIE fighters swarmed around, firing relentlessly.

"Prepare to make the jump to lightspeed," Han instructed.

"Sir?" queried C-3PO.

Han ignored him. Placing his hand on a lever he said, "Watch this!" He pulled the lever back but nothing happened.

"Watch what?" asked Leia.

"I think we're in trouble," Han groaned.

"That's what I've been trying to tell you," interrupted C-3PO. "I noticed that the hyperdrive has been damaged. It's impossible to make the jump to lightspeed."

"We're definitely in trouble," sighed Han.

He climbed from his seat to attempt to repair the hyperdrive, then felt something hard hit the ship. "That was no laser blast!" he cried, running to the flight deck. "Something hit us!" They were in an asteroid field. Han sat at the controls.

"You're not actually going to fly into an asteroid field?" Leia asked incredulously.

"Why not? They'd be crazy to follow us there."

With skill and precision, Han manoeuvred the *Falcon* between the huge chunks of flying rock. Eventually, he saw a massive cavern opening from one of the asteroids. Taking his chance he swerved the ship into the gaping hole.

Can you help Han fly through the asteroid field to the cavern without hitting any asteroids or meeting TIE fighters?

CAVERN

Approaching Dagobah, Luke checked his scanner. "I'm not picking up any cities or technology," he said to Artoo. "Massive life form readings, though."

His X-wing had to carve a path through dense trees and undergrowth as he flew down towards land. Luke hung on tightly as the ship crashed its way through. Artoo screamed from the rear. Eventually, they landed, splashing into swampy water.

Luke stepped from the cockpit and looked around. The X-wing was half-submerged. He appeared to have landed in a jungle. The area was overgrown with trees and creepers, and in the distance he could hear the eerie cries of invisible creatures.

How was he supposed to find Yoda here?

Vader was putting his black helmet over his head when the admiral approached. The admiral watched in silence for a moment until Vader turned around.

"Our ships have sighted the *Millennium Falcon*. It has entered an asteroid field. We can't risk our ships…"

Vader interrupted him. "Asteroids do not concern me, Admiral. I want that ship. No excuses."

There are six words hidden in the grid – one in each column. Each is a four letter name or place. When you have unscrambled all of them, use the leftover letters to spell out a Galactic evil?

1	2	3	4	5	6
U	P	D	A	R	E
E	I	I	E	O	H
K	L	Y	T	S	H
M	E	O	T	L	T
L	A	A	A	O	O

The Empire started bombing the asteroid field in an attempt to flush out the *Millennium Falcon*.

On board the *Falcon*, in the core of the asteroid, Leia could feel the effect of the attack. The ship shuddered with each distant explosion.

"Do you wish to shut me down, sir?" asked C-3PO in alarm.

"No," said Han. "I need you to talk to the ship's computer to find out what's wrong with the hyperdrive."

Suddenly, the ship shook violently. Everyone clung on until the shuddering stopped.

"It's quite possible this asteroid is not entirely stable," said C-3PO.

Han had had enough! "Chewie, take the professor through the back and plug him into the hyperdrive."

Luke removed as much as he could from the X-wing and stowed it at the edge of the swamp. "Now all I have to do is find Yoda. This is a strange place to find a Jedi Master. It gives me the creeps. I almost feel like…"

A voice interrupted him. "Like what?" it said. Spinning round sharply, his blaster aimed to fire, Luke came face to face with a small creature in a cloak, carrying a crooked stick.

"Like we're being watched," he said.

"Away put your weapon. I mean you no harm. Why are you here?" the creature asked.

"I'm looking for a great warrior…a Jedi Master."

"You seek Yoda," said the creature. "Take you to him I will."

A n image of the Emperor appeared. Darth Vader knelt down before his master.

"There is a great disturbance in the Force," hissed the Emperor.

"I have felt it," Vader replied.

"We have a new enemy – Luke Skywalker. He could destroy us."

"He's just a boy," said Vader. "Obi-Wan can no longer help him."

The Emperor didn't seem to agree. "The Force is strong with him. He must not become a Jedi."

"If he could be turned, he could become a powerful ally," Vader observed.

"Yes," the Emperor agreed. "He would be a great asset."

Shade in the boxes listed, then use the remaining letters to spell the name of the Emperor.

	A	B	C	D	E
1		P	R	S	W
2	A	C	O	L	D
3	W	P	A	P	A
4	N	T	M	H	I
5	N	J	T	E	S

Shade in: 3D, 4A, 2B, 1A, 3E, 5C, 4D, 2C, 1D, 3A, 4C, 1E, 2E, 5B, 5E, 1C

Sitting inside the small creature's home, Luke felt cramped and uncomfortable. Outside it was raining hard, and he was frustrated.

"How will I find Yoda here?" he said, setting down his bowl of food. "I'm wasting my time."

The creature sighed and spoke. "I cannot teach him. The boy has no patience. Much anger."

The voice of Obi-Wan spoke. "Was I any different when you taught me?" Luke suddenly realised that the small creature was Yoda.

"You are not ready," said Yoda. "Too reckless. Too old."

"But I've learned so much," Luke pleaded.

Yoda spoke to Obi-Wan. "Will he finish what he begins?"

"I won't fail you," Luke promised. "I'm not afraid."

Yoda stared at Luke with cold, hard eyes. "You will be," he said gravely. "You will be."

Leia screamed as a winged creature landed on the window of the *Falcon*. Han accompanied her outside to investigate. The ground was soft and mushy. "I've got a bad feeling about this," said Leia. Han fired his blaster. The whole place shook. "Let's get out of here!" he cried.

The *Falcon* flew from its position along a narrow tunnel. Ahead, Han could see a huge gaping mouth and teeth – the mouth was closing. He managed to squeeze the ship through the teeth as the jaws clamped together. That was no cave – they had been inside the belly of a huge creature!

Unscramble the words to find the name of the creature the *Millennium Falcon* took refuge in.

CPSAE GUSL

Yoda clung to Luke's back as he climbed up a vine. He was exhausted, but Yoda continued to train him hard. Everywhere he went, he had to carry the Jedi Master on his back.

"A Jedi's strength flows from the Force. But beware of the dark side."

"Is the dark side stronger?"

"No. It is only more seductive."

"How will I know good from bad?"

"You will know. A Jedi uses the Force for knowledge and defence – never for attack."

> **Yoda has set a test for Luke, to sharpen his mind and help him use the Force. Which two shapes should be inserted into the gaps to complete the sequence?**

Yoda took Luke to a cave. "It is strong with the dark side. In you must go."

Cautiously, Luke entered the cave. Suddenly, a movement caught his eye.

Walking towards him was the menacing figure of Darth Vader. Luke knew what he must do. They fought, their lightsabers buzzing.

Luke sliced Vader down, but the figure exploded in a shower of sparks.

In amazement, Luke watched as his own face loomed at the front of Vader's helmet. This must be a bad omen – if Vader could be seduced to the dark side…so could Luke!

V ader had grown weary of his men's failure and decided to resort to other methods. He had gathered a group of bounty hunters to find Leia, Han and Chewbacca. "There will be a substantial reward for the one who finds me the *Millennium Falcon*. You are free to use any methods you wish, but I want them alive."

One of the bounty hunters nodded. "As you wish," he said.

An Imperial officer approached. "My Lord, we have them."

The *Millennium Falcon* appeared from the asteroid field and approached the Destroyer in a direct line. It swooped past the ship, then disappeared from the screens.

"We've lost them!" an officer said.

What is the name of the bounty hunter who spoke? Each letter has a two-number code.

	1	2	3	4	5
1	S	B	R	T	O
2	W	P	E	M	F
3	T	H	O	G	L
4	B	K	U	S	B
5	C	Q	W	A	P

Code: 21/33/14/45   52/32/41/13

On Dagobah, Luke was concentrating hard on his Jedi training. He was performing a handstand and using the Force to lift rocks with his mind. "Use the Force," encouraged Yoda. "Feel it."

His attention was distracted by his X-wing sinking slowly into the swamp.

"We'll never get it out," sighed Luke. "It can't be done."

"Always with you it can't be done," mocked Yoda.

"I'll give it a try."

"No," snapped Yoda. "Try not. Do. Or do not. There is no try."

Luke stood by the side of the swamp and concentrated. The fighter lifted a little way, then sank back down again. He gave up and sat down sadly.

"It's no use – I can't," he complained. "It's too big."

Yoda closed his eyes. Using the Force, his mind lifted the fighter clear of the water to set it down beside the swamp. Luke was amazed.

Han was pleased. He had fooled the Empire. The *Millennium Falcon* was hidden on the great Star Destroyer; as far as Imperial troops were concerned, the *Falcon* had disappeared.

"The fleet's beginning to break up. They're getting ready to jump to lightspeed," he noted. "If they follow standard Imperial procedure, they'll dump garbage and we'll just float away."

"With the rest of the garbage," interrupted Leia.

"All we have to do then is find a safe port." He consulted the charts. "Lando!" he said. "He's on Bespin. We go back a long way."

"Can you trust him?" asked Leia.

"No...but he has no love for the Empire."

As Han had anticipated, the Star Destroyer released its garbage into space. He detached the *Millennium Falcon* from the side and floated along with it.

Leia kissed him. "You have your moments!" she said. "Not many, but you do have them."

Han waited until the fleet had made the jump into hyperspace before risking starting the *Falcon's* engines. When he was sure it was safe, he set a course for Bespin.

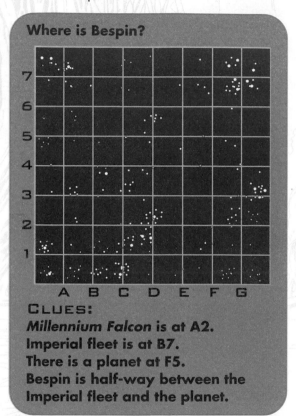

Where is Bespin?

CLUES:
Millennium Falcon is at A2.
Imperial fleet is at B7.
There is a planet at F5.
Bespin is half-way between the
Imperial fleet and the planet.

Behind him, out of sight, a small ship also blasted out of the garbage and followed the *Millennium Falcon*.

While Luke was performing another handstand for Yoda, he saw a vision. "Han! Leia!" he called.

Yoda scolded him. "Control. You must learn control."

"I saw a city in the clouds."

"Friends you have there."

"They were in pain."

"It is the future you see."

"Will they die?"

Yoda concentrated. "Difficult to see."

"I've got to go to them," said Luke.

Can you unscramble the message to find out what Luke has sensed?

AILE NDA NHA REA NI GREDNA.

Han received clearance to land the *Millennium Falcon* on the cloud city of Bespin. When they stepped from the ship, there was no one there to meet them. "I don't like this," said Leia.

"It'll be fine," whispered Han. "Trust me."

A door opened and Lando Calrissian approached them. Han introduced Leia and C-3PO, then Lando took them all into the city. As they were walking past a room, C-3PO stepped inside.

"Who are you?" asked a gruff voice.

C-3PO realised immediately that he had made a mistake.

"I'm so sorry," he apologised.

But it was too late. A blaster blew him apart.

What has C-3PO seen that spells trouble? Starting and finishing on the coloured letter, spell out a name without crossing any line or letter more than once.

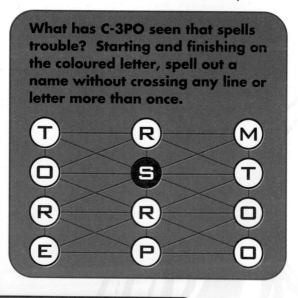

Y ou must not go," said Yoda to Luke. "My friends need me," Luke said. He had already strapped Artoo into the X-wing. "But Han and Leia will die if I don't..."

"You don't know that," spoke the voice of Obi-Wan. "Even Yoda cannot see their fate."

"But I can help them. I can feel the Force."

"But you cannot control it. This is a dangerous time for you. You will be tempted by the dark side of the Force."

"To Obi-Wan you listen," Yoda said.

"I promise to return."

"I don't want to lose you to the Emperor the way I lost Vader," confided Obi-Wan. "Only a fully trained Jedi Knight, with the Force as an ally, will conquer Vader and his Emperor. If you end your training now, if you choose the quick and easy path as Vader did, you will become an agent of evil."

"You not ready," Yoda said. "You need to learn patience."

Ben spoke solemnly. "If you choose to face

Vader, you do it alone. I cannot interfere."

Luke stepped into the fighter. "I understand."

"Don't give in to hate, Luke. That leads to the dark side," warned Obi-Wan.

"I'll return," said Luke. "I promise."

On Bespin, Chewie grabbed the pieces of C-3PO off a conveyor belt. The droid was about to be melted down.

He took the pieces to Han. "You found him in a junk pile?" said Han disbelievingly. Lando Calrissian entered the room. "Why don't you all join us for refreshments," he offered. Leia, Chewie and Han followed him through Bespin to a closed door which Lando opened. Darth Vader was in the room. Han instantly drew his blaster and fired. Vader deflected the shots with the palm of his hand. Stormtroopers appeared and surrounded the group.

"We would be honoured if you would join us," Vader said.

Han looked angrily at Lando. He had been betrayed.

"I had no choice," Lando explained. "They arrived right before you did."

I n the cells, Chewie tried to put C-3PO back together. He slotted his head on backwards.

The droid came to life. "We're in danger," he said. "I must tell the others."

M eanwhile, Vader was torturing Han. Lando stood outside the room, listening to the screams of his friend.

Eventually, Vader came out. He spoke to Boba Fett, the bounty hunter who had tailed the *Millennium Falcon* from the Star Destroyer in his small ship. "You may take Captain Solo to Jabba the Hutt after I have Skywalker."

Lando confronted Vader. "What about Leia and the Wookiee?" he asked.

"They must never again leave this city."

Lando became angry. "That was never a condition of our agreement," he argued.

"Perhaps you feel you're being treated unfairly?" asked Vader.

Lando backed down. He knew Vader had the power to do what he liked. Vader turned and left.

"This deal's getting worse all the time," hissed Lando furiously. Vader was treating him like a fool.

Stormtroopers dumped Han in a cell and left him. Leia and Chewie were with him. When Lando appeared, Han was not pleased to see him.

"Listen to me," said Lando. "Vader doesn't want you at all. He's after somebody called… Skywalker."

"Luke?" Leia said.

"Lord Vader has set a trap for him. He's on his way here right now."

The penny dropped. "And we're the bait," Han realised.

Vader had received good news.
"Lord Vader. Skywalker is
approaching."

"Good. Monitor him and allow him to land. He
must come here."

He looked down at the carbonite chamber.
"When Skywalker arrives, this chamber will
freeze him for his journey to the Emperor. But
first, we'll test it on Captain Solo."

Han was brought into the room. Leia and
Chewie followed him. C-3PO was strapped to
Chewie's back.

Vader wasted no time. The stormtroopers fixed
Han in place. Chewie howled, and struck out at
the guards. Han calmed him down. "I need you
to look after the princess." The giant Wookieé
looked down at Leia.

Han was dropped into the chamber. His face
contorted as the atmosphere around him froze
and he became encased in carbonite.

Turning to Boba Fett, Vader said, "He's all yours,
bounty hunter. Reset the chamber for
Skywalker."

L uke arrived on Bespin with R2-D2. Carefully, blaster in hand, he found his way along the corridors. Escorted by stormtroopers, Leia and Lando spotted Luke. The stormtroopers opened fire immediately. Leia was led away but she managed to shout a warning. "It's a trap, Luke!"

Can you help Luke work his way through Bespin to find Vader?

Cautiously, Luke entered the room with the carbonite chamber. Darth Vader was waiting for him. He stood, tall and menacing, on a set of steps.

Luke slowly climbed up towards him. Vader engaged his lightsaber and it sparked into life.

"The Force is with you, young Skywalker, but you are not a Jedi yet."

Vader attacked swiftly.

Only one of these silhouettes matches the main picture exactly. Can you spot which one?

A

B

C

D

Held captive, Lando, Leia and Chewie were led to Vader's ship. Lando pressed a button on his wrist control – an ambush! His men attacked and soon defeated the surprised stormtroopers.

When they were safe again, Chewie attacked Lando for betraying them.

"There's still time to save Han," Lando spluttered, as Chewie's fingers tightened around his throat.

Meanwhile, Boba Fett stood beside his ship, *Slave I*. He issued an order. "Put Captain Solo in the cargo hold."

Lando, Leia and Chewie rushed to Fett's ship, but they arrived too late. As they ran on to the docking bay, *Slave I* blasted into the sky, with the frozen Han on board.

Vader knocked Luke's lightsaber out of his hand and forced him backwards.

"You have learned much, young one, but your destiny lies with me. Obi-Wan knew this to be true."

Luke fell into the carbonite chamber. Vader reached for the switch which would freeze Luke and allow him to be taken to the Emperor. Concentrating hard, Luke used the Force to free himself. He leaped out and retrieved his lightsaber.

"Impressive!" remarked Vader, when he saw Luke's acrobatic feat. "Obi-Wan has taught you well." Seductively, he tried to take Luke to the dark side. "Now! Release your anger, Luke. Only your hatred can destroy me."

They moved to another area. Vader used the Force to attack Luke. Objects shot from the room and flew at him; Luke had difficulty trying to avoid them. Vader's power was strong.

One of the flying objects broke a window. Luke stumbled towards it and fell crashing through.

C hewie and Leia raced towards the *Millennium Falcon*. R2-D2 had joined them, and C-3PO was delighted to meet up with him again. Behind them, stormtroopers tailed closely, firing blasters.

R2-D2 plugged into the computer. The doors opened, revealing the *Millennium Falcon*.

The door codes have been changed. R2-D2 quickly has to discover the two numbers which will let them through. Insert the correct numbers in the blank boxes and then use the two in the circle to open the doors.

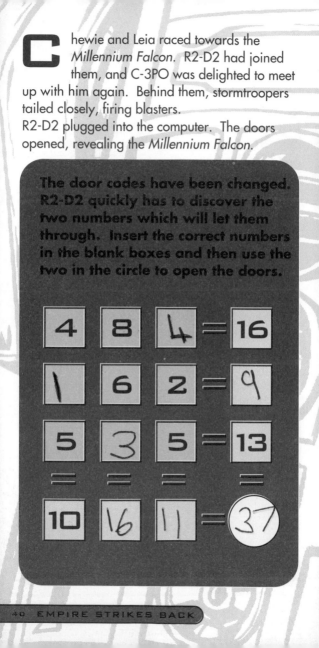

4	8	4	= 16
1	6	2	= 9
5	3	5	= 13
=	=	=	=
10	16	11	= 37

High on a narrow bridge, Luke curled into a ball; he was racked with pain. Vader was defeating him. His dark silhouette towered over Luke. "Join me and I will complete your training. With our combined strength, together we can rule the galaxy."

"I'll never join you," declared Luke.

"If you only knew the power of the dark side," tempted Vader.

Luke moved further away. He was aware of the long drop from the bridge. Still Vader went on. "Obi-Wan never told you what happened to your father."

"He told me you killed him."

"I am your father, Luke."

"That's not true!" Luke yelled.

"Search your feelings. You know it to be true."

Luke screamed in anger.

"Join me, Luke," coaxed Vader. "Together we can rule the galaxy as father and son."

Luke made his decision – rather than join the dark side, he jumped.

He fell a long, long way before landing in a shaft. He slid until the shaft opened up beneath him, then dropped through the gap and landed outside, clinging to an aerial.

Before Vader was seduced by the dark side of the Force, he had a different name. Can you figure out what it was? (Clue: read only alternate letters.)

RAFNTABKUISNO SGKHYJWLATLFKLEPRS

Hanging on tightly, Luke called for Ben. There was no answer. Then he tried Leia. "Leia!" he cried. "Leia!"

Back in the *Millennium Falcon*, Leia felt something. The ship was escaping from Bespin. She suddenly realised what she felt.

"Luke!" she said. "We have to go back."

Chewie turned the ship around.

As they approached Bespin, Lando noticed a figure clinging to the outside.

"It's Luke," said Leia. "Chewie, slow down!"

Chewie manoeuvred the ship underneath him. Lando opened a hatch and pulled Luke inside.

Imperial fighters attacked the *Falcon*. Lando
tried to make the jump to lightspeed but still the
ship failed to reach hyperspace.

On the bridge of his Destroyer, Vader spoke to
one of his officers. "Did your men deactivate the
hyperdrive on the *Millennium Falcon*?"

"Yes, my Lord," said the officer.

On the *Falcon*, Luke lay exhausted. The strain of
the ordeal had taken its toll. R2-D2 tried to
repair the ship.

Vader's voice floated back to Luke. "Join me,
Luke. It is your destiny."

The Imperial fighters closed in, blasting the
Falcon. Vader watched from the bridge. Soon,
he thought, Luke will be captured, and he will
turn to the dark side.

Just then, a blast shook the *Millennium Falcon*. It
threw R2-D2 across the deck – but not before
R2-D2 had made the connection he needed.
Helplessly, Vader watched as the *Falcon* made
the jump to lightspeed. He turned from the
window angrily. His mission had failed.

Once again, Luke Skywalker had escaped.

Safe amongst the Alliance, Luke made a full recovery from his battle with Vader. While Leia comforted him, Lando and Chewie decided to go and look for Han.

"We'll find him," said Lando. "I promise."

Luke spoke to Lando over the comlink. "I'll be waiting for your signal."

The *Millennium Falcon* took off and disappeared. Luke gave Lando and Chewie one final good luck message.

"May the Force be with you…"

Can you make the jump from STAR to WARS in nine moves, changing only one letter each time?

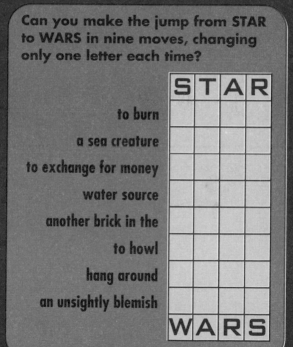

	S	T	A	R
to burn				
a sea creature				
to exchange for money				
water source				
another brick in the				
to howl				
hang around				
an unsightly blemish				
	W	A	R	S

ANSWERS

```
                79
                 T
              41   38
               A     M
           21   20   18
            P    G    F
        12    9   11    7
         B    E    O     X
      8    4    5    6    1
      H    D    A    W    N
```

D	A	G	O	B	A	H
4	5	20	11	12	5	8

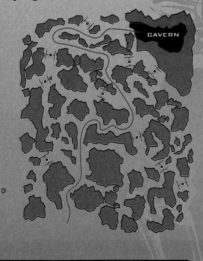

CAVERN

ΠΣ

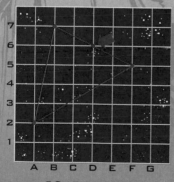

S	T	A	R
S	E	A	R
S	E	A	L
S	E	L	L
W	E	L	L
W	A	L	L
W	A	I	L
W	A	I	T
W	A	R	T
W	A	R	S